Blizzard!

Columbus, OH

SRAonline.com

 SRA

Send all inquiries to this address:
SRA/McGraw-Hill
4400 Easton Commons
Columbus, OH 43219

ISBN: 978-0-07-608793-8
MHID: 0-07-608793-X

1 2 3 4 5 6 7 8 9 NOR 13 12 11 10 09 08 07

The McGraw·Hill Companies

Amanda looked at her checklist for the third time.

"Are you almost ready?" her older sister Jessica asked irritably. "We're waiting." It was a sunny autumn morning, and Jessica was wearing shorts and a T-shirt.

"It might be cold when we get up on the mountain," Amanda said. "Do you have warm clothes in your backpack?" Eleven-year-old Amanda was three years younger than Jessica, but sometimes Amanda felt like the older sister.

"No way, we're just going on a day hike," Jessica said nonchalantly. Jessica had not been enthusiastic, but Amanda had been thrilled when her parents suggested they go on this day hike. Amanda loved the outdoors and had jumped at the chance to get out of their city apartment. She had been at a rustic sleepaway camp all summer and had loved every minute of it.

The best part had been when the campers had had to "survive" overnight in the woods using skills they had learned during the first few weeks of camp. Amanda had learned a lot. She'd even helped build a simple shelter. It had been raining, and the shelter kept everyone warm and dry. The most important lesson she had learned was that she could help herself and others survive in an emergency. Her camp counselor had stressed that they were responsible for themselves but that they also had a duty to help others when needed.

Now Amanda was taking this responsibility seriously. She had made a long list of things to take on the hike, just in case. She had packed a basic first-aid kit, some rope, a flashlight, and other things in her survival kit, which she stuffed in the bottom of her backpack.

Amanda had already packed extra clothes for herself and a hat and mittens in case the temperature dropped up on the mountain. She saw Jessica's fleece sweat suit on the floor next to her bed and stuffed that into her backpack as well, just in case.

"Got everything?" their mom asked, walking into the girls' bedroom. Amanda nodded confidently: Now she was ready.

The drive to the trailhead took about an hour. "Here's the turnoff," Mom said, balancing the road map on her lap.

"It looks as though we'll have the trail to ourselves," Dad said, pulling into the empty parking area. "There won't be any other hikers to get in the way of the fantastic view from the top of the mountain," he added. "We'll be able to see for miles and miles in every direction."

They all got out of the car and headed toward the trail.

"What's a trail register?" Jessica asked, looking at a wooden box nearby. She opened the box and found a notebook filled with names, dates, and times.

"It's a book for hikers to sign themselves in and out, just in case," Amanda explained as she signed them in.

The first part of the hike took them through woods. Dead leaves crunched noisily under their hiking boots, but there were still many red, yellow, and orange leaves clinging to the trees. Some were glistening in the soft sunlight. The trail started to rise, revealing fewer and fewer trees, and suddenly the group was above the tree line on a rocky ridge.

"I'm so ready for lunch," Jessica said. Amanda glanced at her watch and saw that they had only been hiking for about an hour.

"I'm starving, and my backpack is so heavy that it's cutting into my shoulders," Jessica complained. Amanda's backpack was at least twice as heavy as Jessica's was, but she didn't say anything. "Can't we *please* stop and rest?" Jessica said.

"I know you're exhausted, so let's take a break when we reach that rock," Dad suggested, pointing to a huge boulder up ahead alongside the trail. Amanda noticed that the blue markers that identified their trail were painted right onto the rock under their feet instead of on the trees, as they usually were on trails.

Amanda was the first to reach the boulder. She was not racing—it was just that she was fitter than Jessica, who was huffing and puffing behind her. She eased her backpack off and plopped it onto the ground.

"Look at that hawk!" Mom exclaimed, pointing up at the sky.

Looking up at the hawk, Amanda noticed that the sky was no longer the deep cobalt blue it had been when they had started out. Clouds obscured the sun, and a chilly wind blew across the rocky mountainside where they were sitting.

"I'm freezing," Jessica said, her teeth chattering between bites of her peanut butter and jelly sandwich.

"Here, I thought you might need this," Amanda said. She unzipped her backpack and removed her sister's sweat suit. Jessica pulled the fleece outerwear on over her lightweight clothes.

"Good thinking, Amanda," Mom said, smiling.

Amanda zipped up her windbreaker and shrugged her arms through the straps of her backpack. She felt the edge of her survival kit pressing against her back. She adjusted the pack till it was more comfortable.

"I think it might rain," Mom said, looking up at the darkening sky with a concerned expression on her face.

"Rain wasn't in the weather forecast I listened to this morning," Dad said. "It was supposed to be unseasonably warm with a few clouds and little or no chance of precipitation."

"But that was the forecast for home; sometimes the weather up on a mountain is different from the weather down below," Amanda explained.

"Well, aren't you just Little Miss Know-it-all," Jessica teased, grinning and playfully punching her little sister's arm. Jessica had finished dressing and hefted her backpack onto her shoulders.

They continued their ascent, and the trail became steeper.

"How much farther do we have to go?" Jessica asked.

"We're almost at the summit now," Dad said, "and then the trail will loop around to take us back down to the parking area."

"Is that snow?" Mom asked in disbelief. Amanda felt the icy flakes graze her cheek and melt on her skin.

"Yippee, the first snow of the year!" Jessica said, dancing around in a circle with her mouth wide open, trying to catch snowflakes on her tongue.

"Let's keep moving," Dad said, beginning to shiver, "since it's easier to stay warm that way."

"Wouldn't it be great to get enough snow to toboggan down the mountain?" said Jessica. "Now that would *really* be incredible."

"Come on, girls," Mom said.

Amanda could tell that her mother was disturbed by the coming weather, and so was Amanda. "Maybe we should turn back," she suggested to her parents.

"It's probably just a temporary flurry," Dad said, "so let's continue for another half hour and if the weather does not improve, we'll turn around then."

Amanda wished it would stop snowing and that the sun would reappear, but she knew that wishing something could not make it happen.

The weather did not improve. *If anything, it's getting worse*, Amanda thought.

"I changed my mind," Jessica said. "I don't love snow anymore; I despise it. My fingers are like icicles." Amanda took her mittens from a compartment in her pack and handed them to her sister.

"Thanks," Jessica said, slipping her cold hands into the warm mittens. "You really thought of everything, didn't you?"

Amanda smiled and was glad she had thought to bring extra clothes for herself and her sister. Even though Jessica sometimes teased her, Amanda knew that everyone in her family counted on each other. Being the youngest, Amanda did not have as many opportunities to show that she could be responsible for others as well as herself.

"We made it to the summit!" Dad shouted, standing next to a small monument with an inscription.

"I thought you said there would be an incredible view for miles and miles in every direction," Jessica said. The snow was falling so hard and fast that there was practically zero visibility.

"I thought we'd have a picnic up here at the pinnacle, but I think we'd better hurry down instead," Mom said.

"Excellent idea, Mom," Jessica said, "but which way do we go?"

Amanda looked down at the ground where snow had already accumulated. It concealed the blue markers that showed them the way. Dad started brushing the snow away with his boot, but they did not know where to look for the blue marks.

The snow was falling faster and harder now, and Amanda had a sick feeling in her stomach. They were going to be all alone on top of a mountain in a blizzard.

"I thought we would follow the trail and loop around, but maybe we should go back down the way we came instead," Dad suggested.

Amanda looked behind her and saw a few outlines where their boots had made imprints in the snow.

"Let's hurry," Dad said, leading the way.

Amanda wished they could run down the mountain. It had taken them only an hour and a half to get to the summit, and if it wasn't snowing so hard, they could probably get down in half that time. Instead they descended slowly over the treacherous snow-covered rocks as the snow continued to accumulate, making each step slippery and even more perilous.

Dad asked the others, "I don't see any more footprints, do you?"

"I can't see anything at all," Jessica said.

"I'm not sure which way to go," Dad said as the wind propelled snow into their faces, stinging their eyes.

"I'm scared," Jessica said, rather upset, "and I want to go home."

"We'll be home soon," Mom said in her most comforting voice. Amanda was not convinced. It was too risky to continue descending the mountain without a path to guide them. One of them could accidentally fall and get terribly injured.

Her father was thinking the same thing. "Maybe we should just stay put until the snow tapers off," he said uncertainly, even though the storm showed no signs of abating.

Amanda had a sudden realization: She was the only one in her family with the survival skills capable of helping them, and it was her duty to take charge.

Amanda had brought her survival kit, just in case, without expecting to have to use it, but now it might just save their lives. She unpacked her backpack and removed four small cardboard boxes from her survival kit.

"What are those?" Jessica asked.

"They are emergency blankets," Amanda said, handing one to each of them and then tearing one open for herself.

"But it's too tiny to be a blanket," Jessica said, incredulous.

"I've seen these advertised in magazines," Dad said. "They reflect body heat so you stay warmer. They were designed for astronauts to use in the space program."

"They also protect from wind, rain, and snow," Mom read aloud from her cardboard box.

"How did you know we'd need these?" Dad asked as he unfolded his blanket.

"I didn't know we would need them," Amanda said, and then described some of the survival training she had had at camp.

"I guess I just felt like it was my duty to use what I learned. I thought that I should take responsibility for myself and help you too," Amanda explained.

The four of them huddled together wrapped in their blankets. Jessica fell silent and closed her eyes almost immediately while Mom and Dad talked softly. They were debating whether they should stay put or attempt to get down the mountain. One thing they agreed upon was that they would all stay together.

Amanda strained her eyes staring at the white scene in front of her, looking for any indication that the storm was passing, but the ground and the sky were the same white color.

"I thought this all was just a nightmare," Jessica finally said. "But it's really happening. Does anyone have anything to eat or drink?" she asked.

They pooled together the remainder of their food and water and ate some of the snacks they had brought.

"I didn't realize I was that hungry," Mom said after she finished her sandwich. "I feel a lot better now."

"So do I," said Amanda with renewed energy. She still felt a sense of duty to use her survival skills to help her family. She knew it was crucial to build a shelter to protect them from the storm, but there was nothing except snow all around them. Amanda had read about people building snow caves, but she had not packed a shovel in her survival kit and she knew from her research that it was impossible to build a snow cave without one.

"I think I see a tree," Jessica said.

Now that the snowfall was lessening a bit, they could see that there was a pine tree only a few yards away. "How could we have missed this before?" Mom asked as they all walked over to the tree.

"We couldn't see anything during the whiteout," Dad replied. "The worst of the storm may be over," he added hopefully.

Jessica asked, "Do you think we're still near the trail?"

"I don't know, but it's too dangerous to try to walk down in the storm regardless," said Dad, "because we could easily get lost or separated."

"Hey, we can use the tree branches and the rope from my survival kit to build a shelter," Amanda said. She showed them how to weave the tree branches into windbreaks.

With the tree trunk for support, they started building a sturdy shelter and packing snow around it for insulation against the ferocious wind.

Building the shelter was a huge task that took several hours, but they were finally done. It was much warmer inside the shelter without the wind whipping around them, and everyone's mood was heightened.

Jessica drank the last of her water from her water bottle. She went outside the shelter, picked up a handful of snow, and brought it to her mouth.

"Don't do that!" Amanda shouted as she stopped Jessica from eating the snow.

"But I'm still thirsty," Jessica said, "and the snow is clean."

"Eating snow can lower your body temperature so much that you could get sick or even die," Amanda said, taking her sister's water bottle and filling it with snow.

"You can die from eating snow?" Jessica wasn't sure she believed this.

"Put this under your jacket, and it will melt soon," Amanda said as she passed her sister the water bottle filled with snow.

"Now that we have sufficient shelter, I think we should wait out the storm and walk down tomorrow," Dad said.

"I agree that it's our best chance," Mom said.

"I'm already sleepy," said Jessica, yawning. They stretched out wrapped in the space blankets to conserve their body heat.

Soon Amanda heard Jessica's rhythmic breathing and knew that her sister was sleeping, but Amanda could not fall asleep. It was pitch-black inside the shelter now that the sun had set, and Amanda was afraid of the dark. She missed the hall light at home that helped her go to sleep.

Amanda felt inside her backpack for the small emergency flashlight she had packed inside the survival kit. It was there, but she did not turn it on. *Suppose I fall asleep with it on and the batteries run out and then we really need it,* she thought.

Amanda felt such a strong sense of duty as the only one with survival skills that she refused to jeopardize her family's safety just because she was afraid of the dark. Even if she did not sleep a wink, it would be worth it to help her family.

It was cramped inside the shelter, but their body heat inside the space blankets kept everyone warm enough to sleep. Amanda listened to her dad snoring softly. She felt grateful to be alive and grateful for her family. These thoughts helped to distract Amanda from the dark, and she eventually fell asleep too.

"What's that noise?" Jessica asked sleepily.

"It sounds like a helicopter!" Mom and Dad scooted out of the shelter before Amanda was even sure she was awake. She heard them yelling and climbed out of the shelter to join them.

It was early morning with the sun floating just above the horizon, but the sky was bright blue. The snow had stopped overnight.

All four of them ran away from the shelter into an open area where the helicopter pilot would be able to see them. Amanda took off her red windbreaker and waved it overhead like a banner.

"They see us!" Jessica shouted jubilantly. "They see us! We're rescued!" Jessica grabbed Amanda and twirled her around till they both collapsed in the snow, laughing.

The helicopter landed nearby on an exposed patch of flat rock. "Is everyone okay?" a rescue worker asked as she disembarked from the helicopter carrying a large first-aid kit.

"We're all fine," Dad said.

"Thanks to Amanda," added Jessica, giving her little sister another squeeze.

The rescue worker helped them each into the helicopter. "We saw your car in the parking lot and wondered if you were stuck up here," she said. "It was a good thing you signed the register and stayed on the trail."

"It was a good thing our daughter knew some survival skills," Mom said and told them how Amanda had helped them stay alive.

"Sounds like she might like a career in search and rescue when she grows up," the pilot said with a grin.

The helicopter rose up into the air. The machinery made too much noise for them to have a conversation, but Amanda was not feeling talkative. She was thinking about teaching her family some survival skills and planning what she would need to pack in her kit for the next family outing.

Vocabulary

irritably (ir´ i tə blē) (page 3) *adv.* In an angry or impatient way.

glistening (glis´ ən ing) (page 6) *adj.* Shining with reflected light.

fitter (fit´ ər) (page 7) *adj.* Healthier; in better physical shape.

disturbed (dis tûrbd´) (page 10) *adj.* Upset or confused.

descended (di send´ əd) (page 13) *v.* Past tense of **descend:** To come down.

designed (di zīnd´) (page 15) *v.* Past tense of **design:** To create.

task (task) (page 19) *n.* A piece of work to be done.

distract (dis trakt´) (page 21) *v.* To draw one's attention away from what one is doing or thinking.

Comprehension Focus: Making Inferences

1. Based on her actions in the story, what can you infer about how Amanda feels about her family?

2. What can you infer about hiking in the mountains from this story?